Love's Second Chance

a Delta Force romance story
by
M. L. Buchman

Buchman Bookworks

Other works by M.L. Buchman

Firehawks

MAIN FLIGHT
Pure Heat
Full Blaze
Hot Point
Flash of Fire
Wild Fire

SMOKEJUMPERS
Wildfire at Dawn
Wildfire at Larch Creek
Wildfire on the Skagit

Angelo's Hearth
Where Dreams are Born
Where Dreams Reside
Maria's Christmas Table
Where Dreams Unfold
Where Dreams Are Written

Eagle Cove
Return to Eagle Cove
Recipe for Eagle Cove
Longing for Eagle Cove
Keepsake for Eagle Cove

Deities Anonymous
Cookbook from Hell: Reheated
Saviors 101

Get a free Starter Library at:
www.mlbuchman.com

Don't Miss a Thing!

Sign up for M. L. Buchman's newsletter
today
and receive:
Release News
Free Short Stories
a Free Starter Library

Do it today. Do it now.
http://www.mlbuchman.com/newsletter/

1

"You really stepped in some shit this time, Alejandra Martinez." She didn't even know where to direct her fire. Or if she should fire at all.

Lying prone on the roof of the highest building in the area, a whole two stories, gave her the best vantage of the cesspool that had been her hometown for over twenty-five years. US-Mexican border towns sucked, especially when they were on the Mexican side. But she'd never found a way to leave it.

If she started shooting over the low parapet of aged adobe, they'd know she was up here and that could start to suck really fast. Of course another couple of hours up here in the midday sun baking her butt on an adobe grill and maybe she would be ready to shoot all of the assholes who had conspired to trap her up here. They'd gotten blood on her new jeans and sneakers, which was really pissing her off. At least it wasn't hers.

"Next time you're stuck in a street war and trying to survive, remember to bring milk and cookies. Or at least some water." Good reminder, if she ever got out of this one. A six of cold beer sounded good too.

Life had been so much simpler twenty-four hours ago. She'd had a lover, a lousy-as-shit job—making it only a little better than her lover—and something that sort of resembled a place to be.

Now she had a cartel war surrounding the building she lay on top of, and her job was dead—her former employer had owned most of the blood she was wearing. Too bad her job had been to protect his stupid ass. He'd not only been stupid enough to piss off the Alvarado cartel that controlled all the contraband traffic through this town, he'd neglected to tell her he was also setting up the street gangs for a hard fall. They'd found out. Everyone wanted him dead and it was hard to blame them.

The steady crack of automatic gunfire and the hard thwaps of bullets impacting on stone and metal echoed up and down the streets below. These guys were using ammo like it was free. As far as she could tell they were either fighting over who got to claim taking the idiot down, or they were having a gunfight just for the hell of it.

"This town is really going down the toilet."

"Wasn't all that impressive to begin with," a deep voice resonated from close behind her.

As she swung around, a big hand grabbed the barrel of her rifle, stopping it halfway to its new target.

There'd been no sound.

No warning. Not a creak or shift of the rotten roof timbers.

A big *muchacho* knelt close behind her on the roof. He was loaded for action. He held a combat rifle in one hand and her rifle barrel in the other as calmly as if it was the other end of an umbrella or something. Despite his light jacket she could see a pair of Glock 19s in twin shoulder holsters and would wager he had more ammo and another hidden carry or two on him.

A glance past him—the roof access hatch was still closed and latched.

"How the hell did you—" But then she recognized him and knew. "Hector Garcia? Haven't seen your pretty face since Marina was still a virgin." Which was close enough to never. Her little sister had probably seduced her first boy from side-by-side bassinets at the hospital and hadn't slowed down since. At times it was hard to tell if she was a whore or just a slut.

Actually, Hector's wasn't a pretty face, not even the part that wasn't covered by his wrap-around shades and a scruff of three-day beard that looked good on him. He'd broken his nose twice that she knew of, and now maybe a third time by the look of it. She still remembered the knife fight that had earned him the wavering scar from jawline to temple. His dark hair was long, the way he'd worn it ever since he'd lost an ear during a street brawl. He might be a mess, but Hector also looked really good. He used to be one of those slender and dangerous types.

Now he was a powerfully wide and dangerous type.

And at the moment…she must look like shit. *Just perfect.*

She'd been riding *guarda* on a candidate for congress presently bleeding out in the middle of the plaza. What *idiota* campaigned in favor of building a wall on the Mexican side of the border to stop drugs and illegal emigration? That was American-style craziness. But he'd paid her more than she could make anywhere else even marginally legal—which meant he was also on the take in a dozen different ways and worried about it. She could have defended him against one or two shooters. But the two gangs duking it out on the streets below had brought them to his speech by the truckload. She'd dropped four before her sense of self-preservation kicked in.

Now Alejandra was really pissed about the blood on her. She'd also crawled through a shattered luncheon buffet on her way up to the roof. Total mess.

Not usual at all for her to think about how she looked in the middle of a gunfight, but she and Hector had a past—even if it was a long-ago past—and her last shred of vanity had been drowned in reeking mole sauce and blood.

He let go of the barrel and she sat up to get a better look at him.

"Shit, woman!" He placed a big hand on top of her head and shoved her back down onto the roof.

Moments later a single bullet cracked by overhead. She'd drawn exactly the kind of attention she hadn't wanted.

Hector rose quickly onto one knee, then swung his rifle up so fast she could barely follow it. No time to aim. No time for anything. He just fired: two shots, a hesitation with a slight shift upward, then a third. He dropped back down. "That should take care of that."

She had been a shooter of one form or another ever since she was little: possum as a kid, armadillos to put meat on the table after Dad had bugged out, and bad guys as a policewoman—until the drug lords made that too dangerous a beat. But she'd never seen anything even close to what Hector had just done. He'd barely even looked for the target. Maybe the sound of the bullet had been enough. Maybe for him. And she knew if she tracked down the corpse—for she had no doubt that's all it was now—it would have two holes close together in the chest and one more in the head.

There was certainly no return shot whistling aloft from below.

"Sorry," she should have stayed down.

"*De nada!* So," Hector lay on the roof beside her. "You busy much?"

"You saw the body in the plaza?"

"Yeah."

"That was my meal ticket. No major loss—wasn't much of a lover either."

Hector's face darkened at her second statement.

She swung the butt of her rifle into his gut, aiming between a pouch of ammo and a Glock 19. She caught him hard enough to earn her an angry grunt.

"You been gone, hombre. You don't get to judge shit."

He shrugged one shoulder in agreement, but didn't look much happier about it.

Well, neither was she. Especially not with Hector Garcia lying just inches away to remind her of how good her best lover ever had been.

The gunfire down on the plaza was dying down. Probably running out of ammo at the rate they were using it.

"Why? You got any bright ideas on how to keep me busy?"

"More than few," his easy leer said plenty. But she still knew him well enough to know that sex wasn't the only thing he had on his mind.

2

Hector had remembered Alejandra Rosa Martinez as a total knock-out, but that was nothing compared to what he'd found up on the roof.

He'd come back to his shithole of a hometown for a mission, not looking for her. Not really. In five years his life had totally changed—no reason to assume that hers had stayed the same. Or that she'd be real interested in seeing him. But a few questions about her had led him to the plaza, just as all hell had broken loose.

He hadn't expected to walk into a gunfight,

though four years in the US Rangers and another year as a Delta Force operator had let him see the patterns quickly. There was an obvious hole in the battle running from door to door.

The *policia* were wisely hanging back a couple blocks and waiting it out—though they needed a real lesson about how bullets skipped along concrete walls and he hoped they didn't catch one. It was the reason that war zone photos always showed the US military walking up the center of a street rather than hugging the buildings.

But whatever sides were fighting around the plaza and up on the low roofs, the lack of action from the best vantage point spoke volumes. Somebody held the high ground, which meant they were defending it, but there was no sign they were using it. Someone smart—maybe like Alejandra. He got up to the second story inside the building, leaving only a few broken bones behind him. Not a one of them understood that it would hurt less if they'd just let go of their gun when he was ripping it out of their hands.

At a rear, second-story window, he'd

managed to reach up high enough to loop his rifle's sling over a protruding outside timber and used his rifle as a ladder to haul himself onto the roof. There he'd been confronted by one of the finest asses he'd ever seen.

How Alejandra had gotten even better looking in the years he'd been gone, he'd never know. It shouldn't be possible, but it was true.

"You done here?" he nodded toward the plaza.

"Shit, you think?" her sarcastic tongue hadn't changed one bit.

"Good. Got a job I could use some help on."

"You show up out of the blue after five years and you suddenly need help from me? Hector, you're an asshole. You know that, right?"

"Sure."

She snarled at him.

"Never argue with a lady when she's right," he threw one of her favorite sayings back in her face.

Her growl went deep and feline, but when he belly-crawled to the roof access, she followed.

He unsnapped the latch without making

a sound. She had her rifle ready to aim down when he opened the hatch. With a shake of his head, he warned her off.

He flipped the release and threw the hatch wide.

They both rolled away from it. Moments later, a half dozen wild shots cut upward through the hatch. One shooter. Off center to the right.

He aimed through the roof itself and laid down a short line of fire. Crawling across it earlier, it was clear that it wasn't much of a roof. The rounds punched through easily.

Alejandra did the same from the other side and her angle looked good.

Hector rolled back and dove through.

The shooter was down.

Alejandra dropped in beside him, so close it was hard not to just grab her. With a toe of her boot, she kicked the shooter over. He'd been hit both front and back. She'd always been good, but somewhere along the way, she'd gotten even better.

"Alvarado's eldest. They were both really pissed when I wouldn't marry him. His dad, Miguel, is *not* going to be happy about this."

She nudged a boot against him again, hard to believe he was finally dead.

"Good," Hector offered her a smile. "You can tell Miguel yourself when he finds you in his bed tonight."

"That's part of your plan for…whatever?"

It wasn't, but he'd forgotten how much fun it was to tease her. For a second he thought she might try aiming her rifle at him again and he was ready for that.

Instead she kicked him in the shins. Hard.

3

Whatever Hector was into, Alejandra wasn't interested.

But she was.

They scrounged lunch in the deserted first floor café while the gun battle finished dying off around them. They sat side by side in the cool darkness of the kitchen, their backs against the steel door of the walk-in refrigerator and good visibility of both approaches—each with their rifle across their lap. They'd found cold beer, but Hector had opted for water so she'd done the same.

"Where the hell did you go, Hector?"

"North." The only thing north was the US. "Why?"

His frown said he didn't like that question. Not a bit.

She finished her empanada then nudged his ribs with the butt of her rifle.

"You told me to go. Said you'd kill me if you ever saw me again," his face said that his second empanada tasted like bitter sand. He chucked it under the sink.

Alejandra thought back to the day he'd gone. She'd been furious with him for something, then he'd bugged out and she never had a chance to take it back. What was…

Marina! Her slut of a sister had bragged about taking down Hector.

"You weren't supposed fuck my sister while you were with me."

"Didn't."

She opened her mouth, then shut it again. One thing about Hector, he never lied. He might keep his trap shut, but he never lied.

"Pissed her off some that I wouldn't."

Whereas her little sister always lied about everything—and Alejandra always fell for it. Big sisters were supposed to trust their little sisters. But she'd described certain things about Hector that only a lover would know… or someone who'd spied on him making love. "Shit! I'm gonna strangle the little bitch."

Again Hector's indifferent shrug.

"So I tell you to go and you just do? No argument?"

"You had a .357 revolver aimed at my crotch. I'm not gonna argue with that. I know how good a shot you are."

"And you don't even try to come back?"

Hector looked over at her with those sad, puppy-dog eyes of his. She'd never been able to resist those. Six foot of tough hombre was not supposed to have window-to-his-soul kind of eyes, but he always had. "Without you, I had nothing here."

And he hadn't. His family made hers look like all the good bits of a Thalía telenovela.

"Five years." Somehow they'd lost five years. "Five goddamn years."

4

Hector leaned his head back against the refrigerator door and closed his eyes. Yeah, he'd abandoned her to this hell for five years. If she'd done it to him, he'd never forgive her. Shit.

Closing his eyes didn't help.

Now he wasn't seeing her long flow of softly curling black hair with just a hint of her grandmother's dark gold, framing that perfect face. He couldn't see the proud curves above her slender waist that he had so loved to bury his face in. But he could smell her: rich, dark, spicy—overlaid with drying mole sauce on her tight jeans. Like a mix of the lush bounty of the goddess Mayahuel and the fierce and deadly earth goddess Tlaltecuhtli. She had seemed that way ever since they'd sat side by side in *primaria* school desks and learned about the ancient Aztecs.

And she was still that even now, squatting in a darkened kitchen waiting out the stupid shit going on outside: lush, dangerous, and so goddamn good to look at.

He'd landed his fair share of bar babes over the years. His ugly excuse for a face drew in as many as it put off. Not a one had been worth even half of Alejandra Rosa Martinez.

He shouldn't have tracked her down; it was just messing with his head. She wasn't essential to the mission—though it was a better angle than the one he'd thought up while planning back at Fort Bragg. His assignment was to investigate and assess, then call for what assets he needed. If he shifted his plan to include Alejandra, he had all he needed right here.

Reading the profile on cartel boss Miguel Alvarado had brought up too many memories, too much anger. He shouldn't have taken the assignment.

Missions can never become personal. The commanders of Delta Force had beat that into his head again and again. Yet this time it was. His hometown. His family that had been destroyed. And now, in a file handed to him like a random draw, he knew why.

But he *had* tracked her down.

He thumped his head back against the refrigerator door.

Just walk away, Hector. You did it to her before, you can do it again. It's safer that way. Better for her. Sucks totally for you. But since when was that anything new?

Even knowing the right course of action, Hector knew he didn't have the strength to do it again. She was all the past he had. There was no way she could fit into his current life—she wasn't exactly the patient housewife sort—but there was no way he could stand to pry her back out of his heart now that he'd found her. Not that he'd ever been able to.

"So, what's Alvarado up to this time—other than gunning down my meal ticket? And why you?" Even her voice—he'd even missed the sound of her voice. He remembered it like yesterday.

Hector sighed. There was no way to resist having her by his side, so he should just give in. Even if it would only be on a mission.

"Miguel Alvarado is known for moving drugs and immigrants across the border. Pain in the ass, but the US has had plenty of bigger fish to fry."

He could feel her shrug as a movement through the cool metal against his back.

"He's gone a whole lot lower—human trafficking for the sex trade—and it's time to shut his ass down."

"Shit!" Her sound of utter disgust said that was news to her. "Why *you?*"

That was actually a hell of a good question. What he'd seen in the file back at Fort Bragg, intel and his commanders had certainly seen as well. His hometown—giving him the best knowledge on the ground. His family—he'd told the stories to the psychologists during induction testing into Delta. That had to be in his files. It didn't take a genius to connect Alvarado and his own family. His family had worked as Miguel's guns until they were picked off one by one. He'd probably have been in the family trade and dead by now too, if not for Alejandra threatening to shoot his balls off. Just him left now.

There was only one thing he'd never told the psychs about, one piece that had remained for him alone.

He opened his eyes and looked at her.

"Because, I'm the best bastard for the job."

5

The best bastard she'd ever known.

And now he was going to be a *dead* bastard if she ever got her hands back on him.

Tonight's plan had sounded so simple as they'd hashed it out. No unconsidered twists and turns. Whatever training Hector had gotten in the US, Alejandra saw it shine out of him. He brought up scenarios and variables like it was fact, not guesswork. His easy confidence had made it comfortable to believe and trust him despite his five-year absence.

She tugged against the heavy ropes tied around her wrists, but all it did was abrade her already sore wrists. His plan had been great—right up to the moment she'd stepped off plan and everything had gone to hell.

"I was *not* supposed to end up in Miguel Alvarado's bed, Hector. That was supposed to be a goddamn joke." But she had. The bedroom in Alvarado's hacienda was lush. Dark wallpaper, leather and mahogany furniture, a massive California king bed with satin sheets…and a tie-down ring at each corner.

She still had her clothes on, but it was a good bet that wasn't going to last.

Hector had been careful not to say anything about his life in America, but she'd listened to what he hadn't said. No mention of wife or kids. No mention of anything except "work". That's all he called it: work. Not like it took magic powers to figure out what that meant.

The US didn't send Border Patrol hombre*s* south of the line. They were tough bastards, but they were strictly by-the-book types. The US military didn't invade friendly countries. He'd shrugged off Miguel Alvarado's drug trafficking the way no DEA agent would and she suspected that if Hector was CIA, he'd feel creepier.

He didn't. Hector cut a solid, steady hole in the world gone to shit.

US Special Operations Forces. Green Beret, Ranger…one of those types. Except they'd sent him in on his own. A true specialist. Now she knew how he shot the way he had. Delta Force. No one else operated alone, could do what he did, and made it look so goddamn easy.

He hadn't just gotten out…he'd gotten *way* out and done good besides.

Alejandra fought back the burning in her eyes. For some brief fantasy moment, she'd thought there might suddenly be a way out for her as well.

She tugged at the rope, knowing it was futile.

Today had also offered a lousy as shit lesson about revenge.

Hector had gone for some supplies he'd stashed out of town—and she'd gone for Marina. If she'd laid low, like he'd said, she wouldn't be here.

Instead, slamming open her sister's door without knocking, Alejandra had found her with a man, of course. Except this one had Marina gagged and was holding a gun on her.

The wide terror of her sister's eyes had made Alejandra hesitate for the wrong second.

Someone grabbed her from behind, and before she could fight him off, Marina's captor had simply cocked the hammer of his pistol and put the barrel against Marina's temple. Then he'd smiled at Alejandra.

Hector had told her what Miguel Alvarado was now into, cross-border human trafficking for the sex trade. She wasn't a damn bit pleased that she and her sister were getting to see that first hand.

The two of them had been herded into an underground holding area with two dozen others. By the light of the lone dim bulb, Alejandra could see enough of their coloring and features to tell that most were Guatemalan or Oaxacan—at least half were underage. Refugees no one would ever miss except for the families back home waiting for news that would never come. In the stuffy, crowded cell, Marina had told her that the man who had captured them had been a pissed off ex-lover, one of Alvarado's men, who she'd dumped for being too rough.

They were the only locals waiting to be shipped off.

"My timing seriously sucks," Alejandra looked once more at her reflection in the mirrored ceiling above the bed. Miguel Alvarado was a kinky bastard.

He'd come to survey his "cargo" earlier. He'd merely grunted when he spotted Marina. But when he'd seen Alejandra, his smile had gone evil. That was how she'd ended up tied to his bed.

So much for hope.

Now it was just a question of how awful the ending was going to be.

Any time in the last five years, death wasn't that unexpected. She'd known her life expectancy in Mexico stank.

But for one brief afternoon, there'd been hope. The loss of that was now doubly devastating.

6

It had taken Hector six hours through the sweltering afternoon and until well past sunset to track Alejandra. He'd lost ten years off his life when someone had finally dared to tell him that she and her sister had been taken away—bound. That had cost him half the time, finding that first step.

No other Delta Force assets in the area, nor any that could be in place fast enough.

He got on the radio with the intel boys, but this wasn't America—security cameras didn't hover above every street corner. However, they had been tracking a pending shipment of women. The challenge was not only to rescue the shipment, but to nail Miguel Alvarado red-handed.

Hector's plan had been to screw up the night's logistics badly enough to force Miguel to take a personal and very visible hand. He was too well connected to turn him over to the Mexican authorities, but once across the border, there were other ways to deal with him. They needed him alive, at least long enough to reveal his whole network.

But now Alejandra was gone and the paths had all led here—the massive hacienda several miles out of town. He'd dumped his beater vehicle in a handy arroyo and run the last few miles overland. The adobe wall around the massive compound was topped with glass shard and razor wire. Miguel had always been a rich bastard, but clearly he'd reached new depths that he'd needed to turn his home into a fortress.

Hector slid into the compound, only having to leave two guards down for the count. No dogs, which was a mistake, though there were ways of dealing with them. Just made his job easier. Miguel used to keep pit bulls, until they'd mauled one of his sons.

Hard floodlights blinded guards and cast hard shadows.

The security cameras within Miguel's compound weren't well placed—there were plenty of blank spots where they could be avoided. But they acted as excellent signposts guiding him on which way to go—the more cameras, the more important the area was to Miguel.

Inside the garage, Hector found a trio of hot sports cars (all red)—including a Ferrari that looked like it would be an awesome ride. Further in were a half dozen heavy pickups and SUVs appropriate for transporting a personal militia, and a battered American school bus.

Even as he watched, he saw a line of women and children being led up to it from some underground cellar, but not onto it. Instead, hatches in the yellow sides were opened up and the women were made to crawl inside.

Everyone knew that school buses weren't set up to carry luggage underneath like a Greyhound. To any but the most careful inspection, it would appear empty except for the driver who was bound to have some "legitimate" excuse for crossing the border.

They loaded the right side first. Just before she crawled into the rearmost compartment, he recognized Marina Martinez. The years had been far less kind to her than they had to her sister. There was still a beauty there, but now it looked hard and strained. She also looked terrified.

He didn't recognize anyone else.

When the guards finished and moved around to load the other side, he slipped up and unlocked the rear hatch.

"Where's Alejandra?"

"Hector?"

He clasped a hand over her mouth to silence her, then repeated his question.

"Miguel took her," she whispered carefully. "You have to save us. You must—"

"Shh. Too many guards here. I'll come for you later." Before she could protest, he lowered the hatch and relocked it.

And there wasn't time to stop the shipment—he had another priority now.

A quick drop-and-roll beneath a black Chevy Suburban was all that saved him from discovery.

He had the beginnings of an idea and

began putting it in place as he slipped deeper into the shadows.

7

Miguel seemed disappointed that she wouldn't scream. His hard slaps only served to piss her off and make her jaw hurt. Fine, as long as he didn't break it—so that she could chew off his face if she got the chance.

He made all sorts of threats and boasts— most having to do with fucking her to death just to teach her a lesson. Apparently rejecting his now-dead son, as well as his job offer to be a shooter for Miguel's illegal operations had really pissed him off. It was hard to tell which had made him angrier.

Too smart to risk freeing her hands or

ankles, Miguel used a steak knife to slice away her clothes.

"First me. Then the knife," he wielded it down near her waist. "Don't worry, Alejandra. It will be fast. I have other business to see to tonight as well."

He stripped and knelt above her. Alejandra braced herself for the worst. She wasn't going to cry or beg, not for Miguel's benefit. There had to be more horrid ways to die, she just couldn't think of what they were. She wouldn't cry for him, but inside, where her heart ached, she would cry for what she and Hector might have had.

She closed her eyes as his hot breath landed between her breasts.

"First, I'm going to—" then he squeaked.

Alejandra opened her eyes and couldn't make sense of what she was seeing.

Miguel's eyes were wide with shock.

In the mirror above the bed, she had a bird's eye view of the baddest, angriest warrior she'd ever seen.

She'd thought Hector had looked heavily armed and badass this afternoon. Now he was something else. A pair of night-vision goggles had been pulled up onto his forehead. He wore a vest that hung with two pistols, dozens of magazines of ammo for both pistols and rifles, as well as grenades and flashbangs. His puppy-dog eyes now belonged to a full-grown Doberman—a really pissed one.

And she couldn't see his rifle, not all of it anyway. The muzzle appeared to be jammed well into Miguel's ass. The angle was such that if Hector fired, the round would miss her, traveling up through Miguel's body and out the top of his head. She might get splattered with his brains.

She was fine with that.

"Lose the knife."

She thought she knew all the moods of Hector Garcia, but she'd never seen him so angry, so focused in her entire life.

Apparently, neither had Miguel. The blade clattered to the floor.

"Sideways, slowly, until you're lying facedown on the bed. You so much as brush against Alejandra and you're a dead man."

Miguel edged carefully away. The rifle moved with him.

"You okay, Alej?"

Ah-lay. A name she hadn't heard in far too long. She couldn't say all of the things that welled up inside her, didn't dare let them out in the world yet. Digging deep, she found something else. "I could do without the goddamn ropes."

Keeping his rifle shoved someplace dark and nasty, he pulled out a big military knife and slashed her bonds.

Her clothes were in tatters. She went and found some others stashed in a dresser: women's, a wide variety, some close enough to her size. *Bastard.*

She came back and picked up the knife Miguel had dropped to the floor and shifted around until he could see her holding it close by his nose.

"How would you like to fuck a knife, Miguel? Be glad to hold it for you. I'll put you down just like I did your rabid dog of a son."

8

"I need information first," Hector had to slow her down. Not that he could blame her. He felt the same way.

To find Alejandra after all these years and then to come so close to losing her again made him sick. What Miguel had planned for her... the fury rose in a wave that threatened to choke him.

But the 75th Rangers had taught him how to rechannel fury, saving it to focus on the battle moment. Then Delta had taught him how to turn hot fury into cold, until it was a finely-honed weapon.

It didn't take long to get Miguel to spill everything: hierarchy, contacts, combinations to safes, and passwords to his computer. He'd tossed Alejandra a recorder and she'd held it close to his mouth to make sure they didn't miss a thing. How she didn't rip his face off in the process was one of the most impressive displays of restraint he'd ever seen.

Before he let Miguel get dressed, he yanked his rifle free, and shoved a small breaching charge for blowing open locked doors up the guy's ass.

"See this?" he held the remote up close for Miguel to see. "One press of the button and you explode from the inside out. We clear?"

Miguel nodded hurriedly.

Hector tossed the control to Alejandra who caught it one-handed, then looked at him thoughtfully but didn't say anything.

On their way back to the garage, the three of them walked as if everything was okay, Miguel imperiously waving guards aside. They made a few stops along the way. A small knapsack was soon filled with the contents of Miguel's safe, though Hector didn't bother with the cash. Instead he left an incendiary for whoever opened it next. They picked up Miguel's laptop and smartphone along the way, dropping them into foil bags to avoid anyone tracking them.

In the garage, the bus and most of the SUVs were gone.

"Tell me you have a plan, Hector," Alejandra had picked up several weapons along the way until she was almost as heavily armed as he was. It looked damned good on her. "My sister's out there somewhere."

Hector loaded Miguel and his files into the trunk of the Ferrari—thankfully he wasn't a big man. Then Hector hit him with enough morphine from his Delta med kit to keep a horse down for a day.

He and Alejandra slid down into the soft, black leather of the bucket seats.

Yes, he had a plan. But he had a mission to finish first.

9

From the start, Alejandra decided that she was really glad that she was on the same side as Hector. He definitely put the bad in badass. And then he kept getting better.

In the Ferrari—which was one of the coolest rides she'd ever had (it grabbed low and yanked her ahead like a sexual shot)— they'd caught up to the bus and the escorting SUVs close to the border station.

Hector had simply waved a hand out the window as they passed, for the SUVs to keep following the bus. He'd slipped in ahead of them all just at the border.

Whatever ID he showed the border guard had certainly gotten his attention. After a few whispered instructions, the guard let the Ferrari and the school bus roll through.

Hector stopped the car before the bus was fully out of the border crossing control lane, trapping it there.

The SUVs had hung back at the last moment, truckloads of armed guards didn't just roll through border crossings.

Hector pulled out a remote control just like the one he'd tossed to her earlier. He had trusted her—trusted her to not kill Miguel unless they needed to, and to do it in an instant if it became necessary. He'd been right on both counts. No one had ever known her as well as he did.

"I didn't want to risk getting them mixed up," then he flipped up the cover on the activation switch of the one he held, offered her an evil grin, and pressed down on it with his thumb.

The three SUVs still on the other side of the border thumped hard, brilliant light shining out all of their windows. Remote control flashbangs.

In moments, the Mexican border patrol, rifles raised, had everyone out of the vehicles and lying on the asphalt, along with a big enough stack of weapons to make sure they spent a long time in prison.

The next moment, their own vehicle and the bus were surrounded by the US Border Patrol.

INS agents gathered up all of the women and children. A very small team in an unmarked black SUV emptied the still-unconscious Miguel and his files out of the Ferrari's trunk. Their eyes had gone a little wide when she handed over the remote trigger on the breaching charge, and told them exactly where it could be found. Then they were gone.

She and Hector turned to watch as the INS began reassuring the frightened women and children. One was handing out blankets, another with water bottles, and even a few stuffed animals for the youngest to cling to.

"Should I give your sister a contact number? Though I'm not sure if someone that sexy should be allowed into the US."

"You *are* a bastard, Hector. I'm the one you're supposed to be calling sexy." But it was hard to put any real heat behind it with the way he was smiling down at her.

Then she thought about it.

Hector was offering to give a contact number to Marina. It would be *his* contact number, to call if Marina wanted to reach *Alejandra*. That meant that whatever happened next, she herself would be with Hector. Discovering that the tiny shred of hope that had nearly died during the evening wasn't so tiny after all just blew her away. That was way better than being called sexy.

"Sure," Alejandra managed after a deep breath to make sure her voice was steady. "She is my sister after all."

He pulled out a slip of paper, wrote his name and a phone number on it and then handed it to her. At his nod, Alejandra stepped into the crowd of women being corralled onto the bus by the INS agents, this time into the seats rather than the hidden compartments.

She couldn't think of anything to say. Some fit of Marina-jealousy had cost her five years of being with Hector. But it would have been five years in the hell that was a Mexican town on the wrong side of the border.

Now, impossibly, she was on the north side of the border next to a top US military soldier. It wasn't up to her to understand how this screwed-up world worked, but she would absolutely make the best of it.

Alejandra handed the slip of paper to her sister. Marina might be a sex-crazed maniac, but she immediately understood what it meant for both of them.

Marina's "Sorry" was the only word that passed between them as they hugged, but it was a long hug and her little sister's smile wished her joy. Alejandra waited until they were loaded and gone, waving as the bus disappeared into the night.

She turned and saw Hector leaning against the hood of the Ferrari, his big arms crossed over his chest. He'd shed his weapons into the trunk. The black t-shirt that had been under his vest showed just how wonderful his chest had become over the years.

Alejandra stepped up until she was standing between his wide-braced feet.

"What's next?"

"East or west? Your choice, Alej." His deep voice was as soft as the darkness.

"What's waiting for us?" He didn't flinch at the *us*. Instead he unfolded his arms and slipped his hands onto her waist. It was the first time they'd touched in five years and it felt as if they'd never been apart.

"To the east about a day's drive is Fort Bragg, North Carolina. If you're interested, my unit is starting a testing course for new inductees in a couple days. I already called in and got you clearance while you and your sister were talking. I swore up and down that you're a shoo-in. Which is a safe bet because you are. The test is brutal, but I got no doubts."

Alejandra leaned up against him and his arms came up around her. It was the best place she'd ever been.

"And to the west?" she could barely speak past how tightly he was holding her.

"About a ten-hour drive out of our way is Las Vegas. They've got these twenty-four hour wedding chapels. Again, if you're interested." She couldn't see his smile because she had her nose buried against his chest, but she could hear it.

Once more that surge of everything she wanted to say to him shot through her. She dug down and sought for something that would keep his ego in line. That would let him know that she wasn't that easy. That he couldn't just sweep back into her life after five years and change everything in a day.

Except he already had. A job, the best lover, a team to belong to. A home. He *had* changed things; he'd made a dream she hadn't even known about come true.

"One question."

"Uh-huh?"

She looked up into his beautiful eyes, knowing now it was something she'd get to do for the rest of her life.

"Ten-hour drive?"

"Uh-huh," he sounded pretty damned pleased with himself at her response pointing them west.

"But isn't that in, like, a normal car? That *is* a Ferrari you're leaning against."

This time he smiled along with his grunt of satisfaction.

She didn't bother answering yes before she pulled his face down and kissed him.

Their love was so big that it didn't need to be said.

About the Author

M. L. Buchman has over 50 novels and 40 short stories in print. Military romantic suspense titles from his Night Stalker, Firehawks, and Delta Force series have been named Booklist "Top 10 Romance of the Year": 2012, 2015, & 2016. His Delta Force series opener, Target Engaged, was a 2016 RITA nominee. In addition to romance, he also writes thrillers, fantasy, and science fiction.

In among his career as a corporate project manager he has: rebuilt and single-handed a fifty-foot sailboat, both flown and jumped out of airplanes, and designed and built two houses. Somewhere along the way he also bicycled solo around the world.

He is now making his living as a full-time writer on the Oregon Coast with his beloved wife and is constantly amazed at what you can do with a degree in Geophysics. You may keep up with his writing and receive a free starter e-library by subscribing to his newsletter at:

www.mlbuchman.com.

Target Engaged (excerpt)
-a Delta Force novel-

Carla Anderson rolled up to the looming, storm-fence gate on her brother's midnight-blue Kawasaki Ninja 1000 motorcycle. The pounding of the engine against her sore butt emphasized every mile from Fort Carson in Pueblo, Colorado, home of the 4th Infantry and hopefully never again the home of

Sergeant Carla Anderson. The bike was all she had left of Clay, other than a folded flag, and she was here to honor that.

If this was the correct "here."

A small guard post stood by the gate into a broad, dusty compound. It looked deserted and she didn't see even a camera.

This *was* Fort Bragg, North Carolina. She knew that much. Two hundred and fifty square miles of military installation, not counting the addition of the neighboring Pope Army Airfield.

She'd gotten her Airborne parachute training here and had never even known what was hidden in this remote corner. Bragg was exactly the sort of place where a tiny, elite unit of the U.S. military could disappear—in plain sight.

This back corner of the home of the 82nd Airborne was harder to find than it looked. What she could see of the compound through the fence definitely ranked "worst on base."

The setup was totally whacked.

Standing outside the fence at the guard post she could see a large, squat building across the compound. The gray concrete building was incongruously cheerful with bright pink roses along the front walkway—the only landscaping visible anywhere. More recent buildings—in better condition only because they were newer—ranged off to the right. She could breach the old fence in a dozen different places just in the hundred-yard span she could see before it disappeared into a clump of scrub and low trees drooping in the June heat.

Wholly indefensible.

There was no way that this could be the headquarters of the top combat unit in any country's military.

Unless this really was their home, in which case the indefensible fence—inde-fence-ible?— was a complete sham designed to fool a sucker. She'd stick with the main gate.

She peeled off her helmet and scrubbed at her long brown hair to get some air back into her scalp. Guys always went gaga over her hair, which was a useful distraction at times. She always wore it as long as her successive commanders allowed. Pushing the limits was one of her personal life policies.

She couldn't help herself. When there was a limit, Carla always had to see just how far it could be nudged. Surprisingly far was usually the answer. Her hair had been at earlobe length in Basic. By the time she joined her first forward combat team, it brushed her jaw. Now it was down on her shoulders. It was actually something of a pain in the ass at this length— another couple inches before it could reliably ponytail—but she did like having the longest hair in the entire unit.

Carla called out a loud "Hello!" at the empty compound shimmering in the heat haze.

No response.

Using her boot in case the tall chain-link fence was electrified, she gave it a hard shake, making it rattle loudly in the dead air. Not even any birdsong in the oppressive midday heat.

A rangy man in his late forties or early fifties, his hair half gone to gray, wandered around from behind a small shack as if he just happened to be there by chance. He was dressed like any off-duty soldier: worn khaki pants, a black T-shirt, and scuffed Army boots. He slouched to a stop and tipped his head to study her from behind his Ray-Bans. He needed a haircut and a shave. This was not a soldier out to make a good first impression.

"Don't y'all get hot in that gear?" He nodded

to indicate her riding leathers without raking his eyes down her frame, which was unusual and appreciated.

"Only on warm days," she answered him. It was June in North Carolina. The temperature had crossed ninety hours ago and the air was humid enough to swim in, but complaining never got you anywhere.

"What do you need?"

So much for the pleasantries. "Looking for Delta."

"Never heard of it," the man replied with a negligent shrug. But something about how he did it told her she was in the right place.

"Combat Applications Group?" Delta Force had many names, and they certainly lived to "apply combat" to a situation. No one on the planet did it better.

His next shrug was eloquent.

Delta Lesson One: *Folks on the inside of the wire didn't call it Delta Force. It was CAG or "The Unit."* She got it. Check. Still easier to think of it as Delta though.

She pulled out her orders and held them up. "Received a set of these. Says to show up here today."

"Let me see that."

"Let me through the gate and you can look at it as long as you want."

"Sass!" He made it an accusation.

"Nope. I just don't want them getting damaged or lost maybe by accident." She offered her blandest smile with that.

"They're that important to you, girlie?"

"Yep!"

He cracked what might have been the start of a grin, but it didn't get far on that grim face. Then he opened the gate and she idled the bike forward, scuffing her boots through the dust.

From this side she could see that the chain link was wholly intact. There was a five-meter swath of scorched earth inside the fence line. Through the heat haze, she could see both infrared and laser spy eyes down the length of the wire. And that was only the defenses she could see. So…a very *not* inde-fence-ible fence. Absolutely the right place.

When she went to hold out the orders, he waved them aside.

"Don't you want to see them?" This had to be the right place. She was the first woman in history to walk through The Unit's gates by order. A part of her wanted the man to acknowledge that. Any man. A Marine Corps marching band wouldn't have been out of order.

She wanted to stand again as she had on that very first day, raising her right hand. "I, Carla Anderson, do solemnly swear that I will support and defend the Constitution…"

She shoved that aside. The only man's acknowledgment she'd ever cared about was her big brother's, and he was gone.

The man just turned away and spoke to her over his shoulder as he closed the gate behind her bike. "Go ahead and check in. You're one of the last to arrive. We start in a couple hours"—as if it were a blasted dinner party. "And I already saw those orders when I signed them. Now put them away before someone else sees them and thinks you're still a soldier." He walked away.

She watched the man's retreating back. *He'd* signed her orders?

That was the notoriously hard-ass Colonel Charlie Brighton?

What the hell was the leader of the U.S. Army's Tier One asset doing manning the gate? Duh…assessing new applicants.

This place *was* whacked. Totally!

There were only three Tier One assets in the entire U.S. military. There was Navy's Special Warfare Development Group, DEVGRU, that the public thought was called SEAL Team Six—although it hadn't been named that for thirty years now. There was the Air Force's 24th STS—which pretty much no one on the outside had ever heard of. And there was the 1st Special Forces Operational Detachment— Delta—whose very existence was still denied by the Pentagon despite four decades of operations, several books, and a couple of seriously off-the-mark movies that were still fun to watch because Chuck Norris kicked ass even under the stupidest of circumstances.

Total Tier One women across all three teams? Zero.

About to be? One. Staff Sergeant First Class Carla Anderson.

Where did she need to go to check in? There was no signage. No drill sergeant hovering. No—

Delta Lesson Number Two: *You aren't in the Army anymore, sister.*

No longer a soldier, as the Colonel had

said, at least not while on The Unit's side of the fence. On this side they weren't regular Army; they were "other."

If that meant she had to take care of herself, well, that was a lesson she'd learned long ago. Against stereotype, her well-bred, East Coast white-guy dad was the drunk. Her dirt-poor half Tennessee Cherokee, half Colorado settler mom, who'd passed her dusky skin and dark hair on to her daughter, had been a sober and serious woman. She'd also been a casualty of an Afghanistan dust-bowl IED while serving in the National Guard. Carla's big brother Clay now lay beside Mom in Arlington National Cemetery. Dead from a training accident. Except your average training accident didn't include a posthumous rank bump, a medal, and coming home in a sealed box reportedly with no face.

Clay had flown helicopters in the Army's 160th SOAR with the famous Majors Beale and Henderson. Well, famous in the world of people who'd flown with the Special Operations Aviation Regiment, or their little sisters who'd begged for stories of them whenever big brothers were home on leave. Otherwise totally invisible.

Clay had clearly died on a black op that she'd never be told a word of, so she didn't bother asking. Which was okay. He knew the risks, just as Mom had. Just as she herself had when she'd signed up the day of Clay's funeral, four years ago. She'd been on the front lines ever since and so far lived to tell about it.

Carla popped Clay's Ninja—which is how she still thought of it, even after riding it for four years—back into first and rolled it slowly up to the building with the pink roses. As good a place to start as any.

***

"Hey, check out this shit!"

Sergeant First Class Kyle Reeves looked out the window of the mess hall at the guy's call. Sergeant Ralph last-name-already-forgotten was 75th Rangers and too damn proud of it.

Though…damn! Ralphie was onto something.

Kyle would definitely check out *this shit.*

Babe on a hot bike, looking like she knew how to handle it.

Through the window, he inspected her lean length as she clambered off the machine.

Army boots. So call her five-eight, a hundred and thirty, and every part that wasn't amazing curves looked like serious muscle. Hair the color of lush, dark caramel brushed her shoulders but moved like the finest silk, her skin permanently the color of the darkest tan. Women in magazines didn't look that hot. Those women always looked anorexic to him anyway, even the pinup babes displayed on Hesco barriers at forward operating bases up in the Hindu Kush where he'd done too much of the last couple years.

This woman didn't look like that for a second. She looked powerful. And dangerous.

Her tight leathers revealed muscles made of pure soldier.

Ralph Something moseyed out of the mess-hall building where the hundred selectees were hanging out to await the start of the next testing class at sundown.

Well, Kyle sure wasn't going to pass up the opportunity for a closer look. Though seeing Ralph's attitude, Kyle hung back a bit so that he wouldn't be too closely associated with the dickhead.

Ralph had been spoiling for a fight ever

since he'd found out he was one of the least experienced guys to show up for Delta selection. He was from the 75th Ranger Regiment, but his deployments hadn't seen much action. Each of his attempts to brag for status had gotten him absolutely nowhere.

Most of the guys here were 75th Rangers, 82nd Airborne, or Green Beret Special Forces like himself. And most had seen a shitload of action because that was the nature of the world at the moment. There were a couple SEALs who hadn't made SEAL Team Six and probably weren't going to make Delta, a dude from the Secret Service Hostage Rescue Team who wasn't going to last a day no matter how good a shot he was, and two guys who were regular Army.

The question of the moment though, who was she?

Her biking leathers were high-end, sewn in a jagged lightning-bolt pattern of yellow on smoke gray. It made her look like she was racing at full tilt while standing still. He imagined her hunched over her midnight-blue machine and hustling down the road at her Ninja's top speed—which was north of 150.

He definitely had to see that one day.

Kyle blessed the inspiration on his last leave that had made him walk past the small Toyota pickup that had looked so practical and buy the wildfire-red Ducati Multistrada 1200 instead. Pity his bike was parked around the back of the barracks at the moment. Maybe they could do a little bonding over their rides. Her machine looked absolutely cherry.

Much like its rider.

Ralph walked right up to her with all his arrogant and stupid hanging out for everyone to see. The other soldiers began filtering outside to watch the show.

"Well, girlie, looks like you pulled into the wrong spot. This here is Delta territory."

Kyle thought about stopping Ralph, thought that someone should give the guy a good beating, but Dad had taught him control. He would take Ralph down if he got aggressive, but he really didn't want to be associated with the jerk, even by grabbing him back.

The woman turned to face them, then unzipped the front of her jacket in one of those long, slow, movie moves. The sunlight shimmered across her hair as she gave it an "unthinking" toss. Wraparound dark glasses hid her eyes, adding to the mystery.

He could see what there was of Ralph's brain imploding from lack of blood. He felt the effect himself despite standing a half-dozen paces farther back.

She wasn't hot; she sizzled. Her parting leathers revealed an Army green T-shirt and proof that the very nice contours suggested by her outer gear were completely genuine. Her curves weren't big—she had a lean build—but they were as pure woman as her shoulders and legs were pure soldier.

"There's a man who called me 'girlie' earlier." Her voice was smooth and seductive, not low and throaty, but rich and filled with nuance.

She sounded like one of those people who could hypnotize a Cobra, either the snake or the attack helicopter.

"He's a bird colonel. He can call me that if he wants. You aren't nothing but meat walking on sacred ground and wishing he belonged."

Kyle nodded to himself. The "girlie" got it in one.

"*You*"—she jabbed a finger into Sergeant

Ralph Something's chest—"do not get 'girlie' privileges. *We* clear?"

"Oh, sweetheart, I can think of plenty of privileges that you'll want to be giving to—" His hand only made it halfway to stroking her hair.

If Kyle hadn't been Green Beret trained, he wouldn't have seen it because she moved so fast and clean.

"—*me!*" Ralph's voice shot upward on a sharp squeak.

The woman had Ralph's pinkie bent to the edge of dislocation and, before the man could react, had leveraged it behind his back and upward until old Ralph Something was perched on his toes trying to ease the pressure. With her free hand, she shoved against the middle of his back to send him stumbling out of control into the concrete wall of the mess hall with a loud *clonk* when his head hit.

Minimum force, maximum result. The Unit's way.

She eased off on his finger and old Ralph dropped to the dirt like a sack of potatoes. He didn't move much.

"Oops." She turned to face the crowd that had gathered.

She didn't even have to say, "Anyone else?" Her look said plenty.

Kyle began to applaud. He wasn't the only one, but he was in the minority. Most of the guys were doing a wait and see.

A couple looked pissed.

Everyone knew that the Marines' combat training had graduated a few women, but that was just jarheads on the ground.

This was Delta. The Unit was Tier One. A Special Mission Unit. They were supposed to be the one true bastion of male dominance. No one had warned them that a woman was coming in.

Just one woman, Kyle thought. The first one. How exceptional did that make her? Pretty damn was his guess. Even if she didn't last the first day, still pretty damn. And damn pretty. He'd bet on dark eyes behind her wraparound shades. She didn't take them off, so it was a bet he'd have to settle later on.

A couple corpsmen came over and carted Ralph Something away even though he was already sitting up—just dazed with a bloody cut on his forehead.

The Deltas who'd come out to watch the

show from a few buildings down didn't say a word before going back to whatever they'd been doing.

Kyle made a bet with himself that Ralph Something wouldn't be showing up at sundown's first roll call. They'd just lost the first one of the class and the selection process hadn't even begun. Or maybe it just had.

"Where's check-in?" Her voice really was as lush as her hair, and it took Kyle a moment to focus on the actual words.

He pointed at the next building over and received a nod of thanks.

That made watching her walk away in those tight leathers strictly a bonus.

Available at fine retailers everywhere.

Other works by M.L. Buchman

Firehawks

MAIN FLIGHT
Pure Heat
Full Blaze
Hot Point
Flash of Fire
Wild Fire

SMOKEJUMPERS
Wildfire at Dawn
Wildfire at Larch Creek
Wildfire on the Skagit

Angelo's Hearth
Where Dreams are Born
Where Dreams Reside
Maria's Christmas Table
Where Dreams Unfold
Where Dreams Are Written

Eagle Cove
Return to Eagle Cove
Recipe for Eagle Cove
Longing for Eagle Cove
Keepsake for Eagle Cove

Deities Anonymous
Cookbook from Hell: Reheated
Saviors 101

Don't Miss a Thing!
Sign up for M. L. Buchman's newsletter
today
and receive:
Release News
Free Short Stories
a Free Starter Library

Do it today. Do it now.
http://www.mlbuchman.com/newsletter/

39499289R00050

Made in the USA
Middletown, DE
17 January 2017